Fribbity RIBBIT!

by Suzanne C. Johnson

illustrated by Debbie Tilley

Alfred A. Knopf • New York

To Allen and Brandon with
much love and gratitude
—SCJ

For Gillian
—DT

THIS IS A BORZOI BOOK
PUBLISHED BY ALFRED A. KNOPF

Text copyright © 2001 by Suzanne C. Johnson
Illustrations copyright © 2001 by Debbie Tilley

KNOPF, BORZOI BOOKS, and the colophon are registered
trademarks of Random House, Inc.

www.randomhouse.com/Kids

Library of Congress Cataloging-in-Publication Data
Johnson, Suzanne C.
Fribbity ribbit! / by Suzanne C. Johnson ; illustrations
by Debbie Tilley.—1st ed
p. cm.
Summary: A frog on the loose in a house causes havoc
and mayhem.
ISBN 0-375-81199-0 (trade) – ISBN 0-375-91199-5 (lib. bdg.)
[1. Frogs—Fiction. 2. Humorous stories.] I. Tilley, Debbie,
ill. II. Title.
PZ7.J6378 Fr 2001
[E]—dc21   2001029615

August 2001
First Edition

Printed in the United States of America

10 9 8 7 6 5 4 3 2 1

Frog
in
my
backyard!

Frog in Dad's garage.
Fribbity-ribbit.
Got him?
Fribbity-rap-rap-rap!
Ribbity-tap-tap-tap!

Frog in Granny's office.

Frog in Sister's bath.

Fribbity-ribbit.

Got him?

Fribbity-splish!

Ribbity-splash!

Eeek!

Frog on Baby's train.

Fribbity-choo-choo!

Ribbity-wooo-wooo!

Aaaaah.

Frog in Brother's room.
Fribbity-twing-twang-toot!
Ribbity-bing-bang-boom!

Yikes!

Frog in Mama's studio.

Fribbity-ribbit.

Got him?

Fribbity-green!

Fribbity-orange!

Ribbity-red, white, and blue!

Hippity-hippity.
     Which way?
Hoppity-hoppity.

That way!

MEEOOOWW!

Fribbity-fribbity-fribbity!

Ribbity-ribbity-ribbity!!

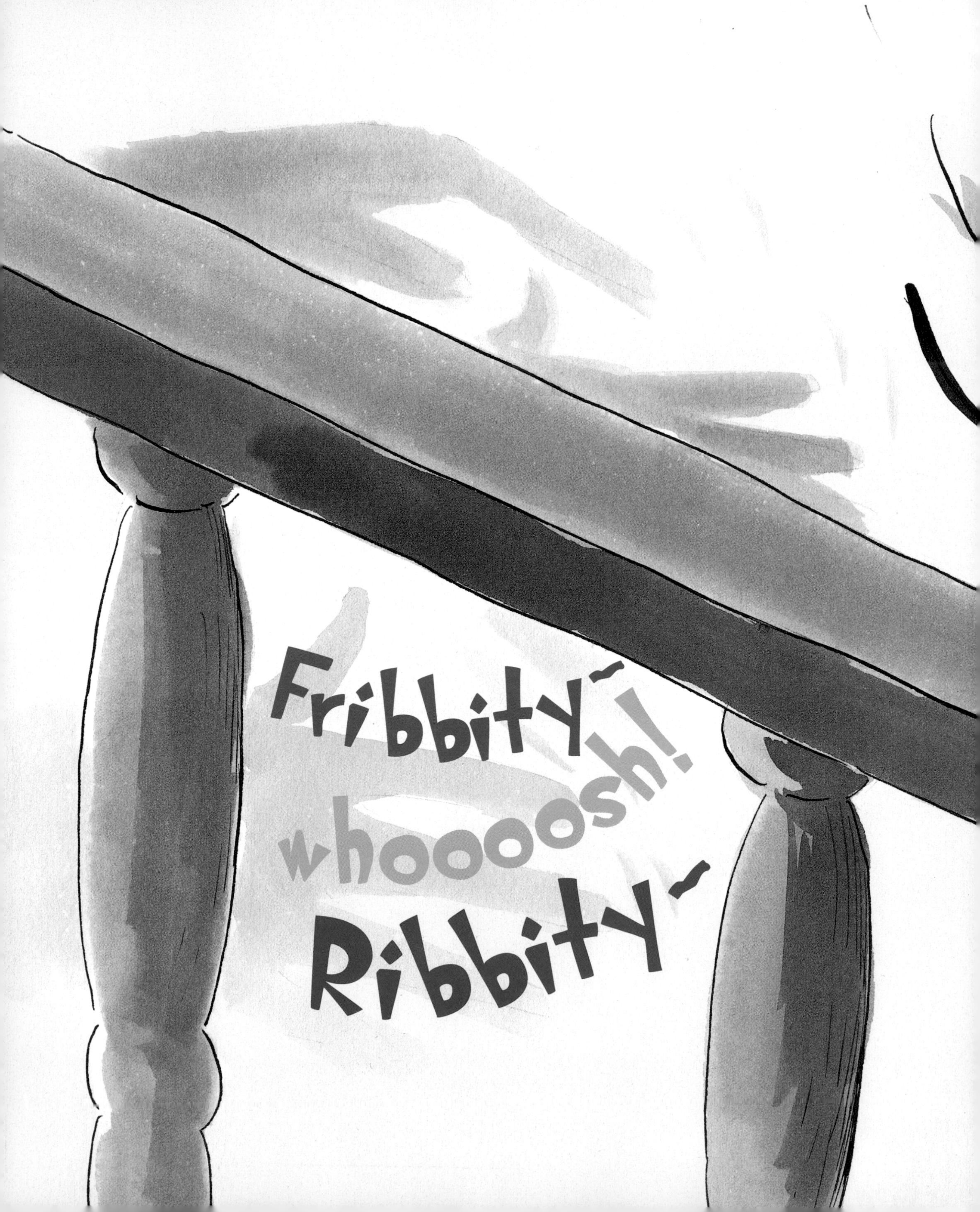
Fribbity-
whoooosh!
Ribbity-

Frog in my backyard!

Fribbity RIBBIT!